I'm Going To R[E]

These levels are meant only as guides;
you and your child can best choose a book that's right.

UP TO 50 WORDS

Level 1: Kindergarten–Grade 1 . . . Ages 4–6
- word bank to highlight new words
- consistent placement of text to promote readability
- easy words and phrases
- simple sentences build to make simple stories
- art and design help new readers decode text

UP TO 100 WORDS

Level 2: Grade 1 . . . Ages 6–7
- word bank to highlight new words
- rhyming texts introduced
- more difficult words, but vocabulary is still limited
- longer sentences and longer stories
- designed for easy readability

UP TO 200 WORDS

Level 3: Grade 2 . . . Ages 7–8
- richer vocabulary of up to 200 different words
- varied sentence structure
- high-interest stories with longer plots
- designed to promote independent reading

MORE THAN 300 WORDS

Level 4: Grades 3 and up . . . Ages 8 and up
- richer vocabulary of more than 300 different words
- short chapters, multiple stories, or poems
- more complex plots for the newly independent reader
- emphasis on reading for meaning

LEVEL 2

2 4 6 8 10 9 7 5 3

Published by Sterling Publishing Co., Inc.
387 Park Avenue South, New York, NY 10016
Text copyright © 2006 by Harriet Ziefert Inc.
Illustrations copyright © 2006 by David Jacobson
Distributed in Canada by Sterling Publishing
c/o Canadian Manda Group, 165 Dufferin Street
Toronto, Ontario, Canada M6K 3H6
Distributed in Great Britain and Europe by Chris Lloyd at Orca Book
Services, Stanley House, Fleets Lane, Poole BH15 3AJ, England
Distributed in Australia by Capricorn Link (Australia) Pty. Ltd.
P.O. Box 704, Windsor, NSW 2756, Australia

I'm Going To Read is a trademark of Sterling Publishing Co., Inc.

Library of Congress Cataloging-in-Publication Data

Jacobson, David.
  Three wishes / pictures by David Jacobson.
    p. cm. — (I'm going to read)
  Summary: A child expresses a morning wish to go fishing, a noon
wish to be "boss of the kitchen," and a night wish to climb the
apple tree outside the window.
  ISBN 1-4027-3130-2
  [1. Wishes—Fiction.] I. Title. II. Series.

PZ7.J15265Thr 2005
[E]—dc22   2005019001

Sterling ISBN 13: 978-1-4027-3130-3
Sterling ISBN 10: 1-4027-3130-2

For information about custom editions, special sales, premium and
corporate purchases, please contact Sterling Special Sales
Department at 800-805-5489 or specialsales@sterlingpub.com.

I'm Going To READ!

Three Wishes

Pictures by David Jacobson

Sterling Publishing Co., Inc.
New York

CHAPTER 1
Morning Wish

I want to fish
in the pond outside.

I want to put my fishing line
in the water.

I want to pull . . .

and pull . . .

and pull.

And, before I'm done,
I want to pull out
two hundred . . .

and twenty-two fishes!

CHAPTER 2
Noon Wish

I want to be
boss of the kitchen . . .

and eat just how I want.

I'll sit at the head of the table.

I'll begin with
raisins and peanuts.

I'll end with french fries and pizza.

And, when I'm done,
I'll throw my napkin away and . . .

window　apple　night　on　tree

wipe my mouth
on my sleeve!

CHAPTER 3
Night Wish

I want to climb the apple tree
outside my window.

I want to climb
the tree at night . . .

piece   get

and get
a piece of fruit . . .

fruit   a

moon

and a piece of moon.

Then I will go to bed,
my pockets full—
one with fruit . . .

then   pockets   bed

and the other
with moon.